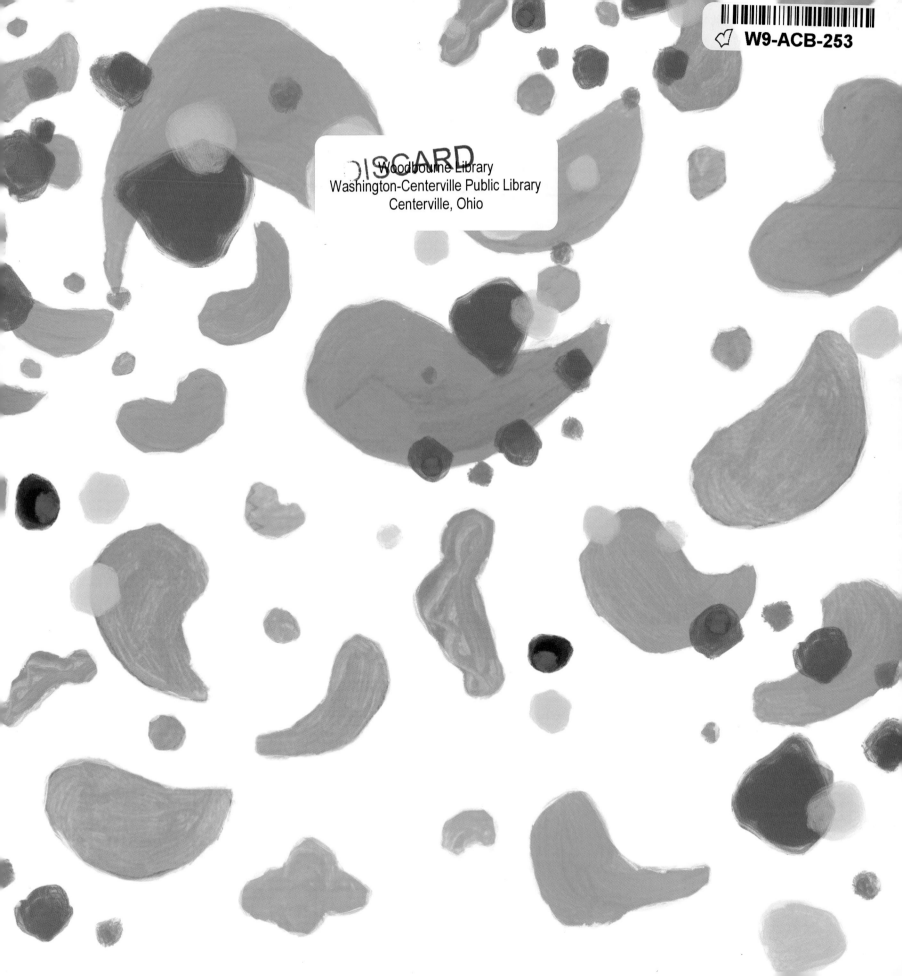

Originally published as *Muizenmuziek* in Belgium and the Netherlands by Clavis Uitgeverij, 2020
English translation from the Dutch by Clavis Publishing Inc., New York

Visit us on the Web at www.clavis-publishing.com.

Mouse Music written by Suzan Overmeer and illustrated by Myriam Berenschot

ISBN 978-1-60537-636-3

This book was printed in February 2021 at Nikara, M. R. Štefánika 858/25, 963 01 Krupina, Slovakia.

First Edition
10 9 8 7 6 5 4 3 2 1

Written by Suzan Overmeer
Illustrated by Myriam Berenschot

Mouse music

Clavis

NEW YORK

Isabel Mouse lives in an old walnut tree
on the edge of the forest.
Isabel can play violin all day long.
She loves to dream about beautiful sounds,
while playing her music.

Isabel has a sister and two little brothers.
All of them make music.
André, Isabel's youngest brother, plays violin as well.
Her sister Lavinia plays the harp, and her brother
Wibi plays piano.
When the four mice make music together,
the other animals in the forest are very quiet
because they don't want to miss anything.

Isabel loves adventure. With her violin
on her back, she walks into the forest every day,
searching for sounds she doesn't even know yet.
Today, she quickly hears something special.
In a maple tree, an unknown bird sings
one beautiful song after another.
Isabel listens, grabs her violin, and plays along.
My brothers and sister should hear this, she thinks cheerfully.

Isabel calls Lavinia, Wibi, and André.
"Listen," Isabel says, "you've never
heard anything like this before!"
She plays along with the bird's song again.
The bird is singing even more beautifully now,
and Isabel's playing gets even better.
"This sounds very different from our music," Lavinia says.
"Our music is much better," Wibi believes.
"This is just a bird singing," André mutters.
Isabel sighs. *Better luck next time*, she thinks.

The next day, Isabel sets off again.

She climbs over
branches and leaves,
and walks along
a forest path.

Step, step, step-step-step.

After a while, she stops to get some rest and to dream.
Suddenly, an ant comes walking along the path.
Behind him, there comes another ant and another one!
Dozens of ants walk past her with brisk steps.

Step, step, step-step-step.

Isabel listens closely, then she takes out her violin,
and plays along with the rhythm of the ants.
My brothers and sister should hear this, she thinks happily.

Isabel calls Lavinia, Wibi, and André.
"Listen," she says, "you've never heard anything like this before!"
Again, she plays along with the rhythm of the ants.
The ants keep stepping and Isabel plays
until the last ant walks past.
"This sounds very different from our music," Lavinia says.
"Our music is much better," Wibi believes.
"These are just ants walking," André mutters.
Isabel says nothing. *Maybe next time*, she thinks.

A couple of days later, it rains.
Isabel leaves her violin at home
and heads to the forest.
She stomps cheerfully through
the puddles, and whistles a song.
All of a sudden, she hears
strange music in the distance.
She goes straight to the sound
until she sees four strange mice.

Isabel hides behind some flowers and listens . . .
The four mice sing together
and one of them plays guitar!
My brothers and sister should hear this,
Isabel thinks excitedly.

Isabel calls Lavinia, Wibi, and André.
"Listen," she whispers, "you've never heard anything like this before!"
Surprised, Isabel's brothers and sister listen to the singing
and guitar playing of the other mice.

"This sounds very different from our music," Lavinia says.
"Our music is much more fun," Wibi believes.
"This is nothing. Can you even call it music?" André mutters.
But the mice hear him, and stop playing as they look around.
Cautiously, the two groups approach each other.

The mouse with the guitar says:
"Hello, I'm Maestro Mouse."
He points at the other three.
"And these are Mina, Mira, and Mila Mouse.
We come from the city, but the people there
leave so much plastic lying around
on the streets that we become sick.
We hope to find more luck here."
"Ah, mice from the city!" Lavinia says.
"That's why your music sounds so weird."
"Weird?" the city mice shout with one voice.
"Very weird," André mutters.
And then all the mice start screaming
at the same time.

Isabel can't bear it anymore.
"Stop!" she screams.

Everyone is silent now.
Then Lavinia, André,
and Wibi walk back into the
forest with their noses turned up.
"I'm sorry," Isabel says quietly.
"I do like your music.
May I keep on listening?"

The city mice nod and start
singing and playing again.
Their voices flow quickly
and merge. It sounds like
the words are dancing!
Isabel listens in awe.
Then she gets an idea.

She quickly trips home to get her violin.
When she's back with her new friends,
she tries to play along.

Isabel lets the sounds from her violin
merge with the voices and the guitar
of the city mice. Soon, marvelous music
can be heard throughout the forest.

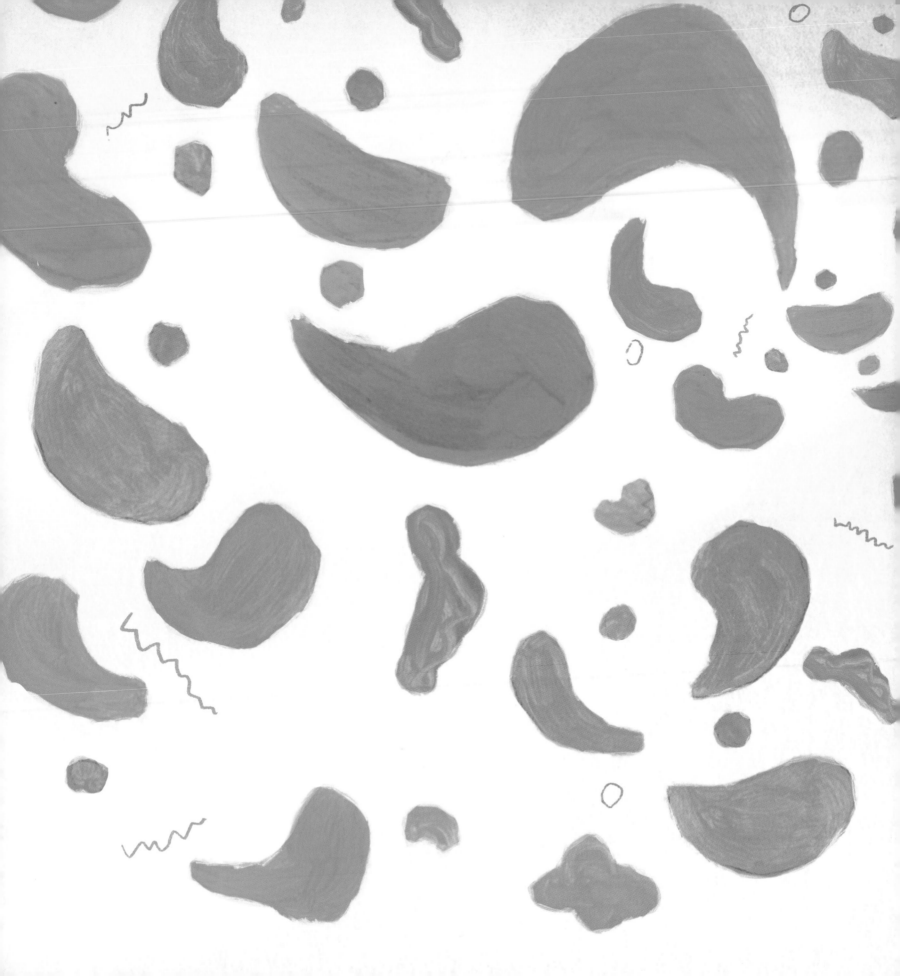

Lavinia, Wibi, and André hear the music as well.
Is Isabel really playing along with those mice from the city?
The three mice look at each other and listen attentively for a while.
They hear how the voices and the instruments fluently merge,
as if they speak a new language.
All of a sudden, the three mice understand how special this music is.
"Shall we go back?" André mutters.
"To apologize?" Wibi asks.
Lavinia nods without saying anything.

When they come up to Isabel and the city mice, it gets quiet.
"Your music sounds different from our music," Lavinia says after a while.
"But what you do is really great," Wibi quickly adds.
"I think it's actually . . . very beautiful," André sighs.
"At last!" Isabel cheers. "Other music is beautiful too, if you listen carefully."
She happily looks at everyone. Then she continues playing with
the city mice, while her brothers and sister listen. Listen very carefully.

Mouse suggestions for musical education

Listening like Isabel

Isabel loves listening.
Can you listen well too?
Close your eyes and be very quiet.
What do you hear?
Do you recognize all the sounds?
What sounds faraway and what
close by? Which sounds do you like?

Singing like a bird

Isabel hears a bird singing in the
forest. Sing a (well known) song together, just like the bird.
One of the children can be Isabel.
With an instrument (for instance
a drum or a woodblock), that child
plays along with the song.
You can play in time, or play along
  with the rhythm or the lyrics of the
        song.
      Who's next to play Isabel?

When there are several instruments,
several children can be Isabel at the
same time.

Stomping like the ants

Ants are walking through the forest.
Isabel hears them stomping.
Can you also make sounds by stom-
ping your feet? Surely you can!
And can you make music doing this?
Bang a drum in a leisurely pace or hit
another rhythmic instrument.
Can everyone stomp along in time?
Change the tempo. You can try be-
ginning slowly and ending quickly.

Making sounds with
your body

Isabel loves sounds! Try to make
sounds with your own body.
You could clap your hands, rub
your legs, click your tongue . . .
Let everyone come up with their
own sound and demonstrate it.
The rest of the group can imitate
that sound.

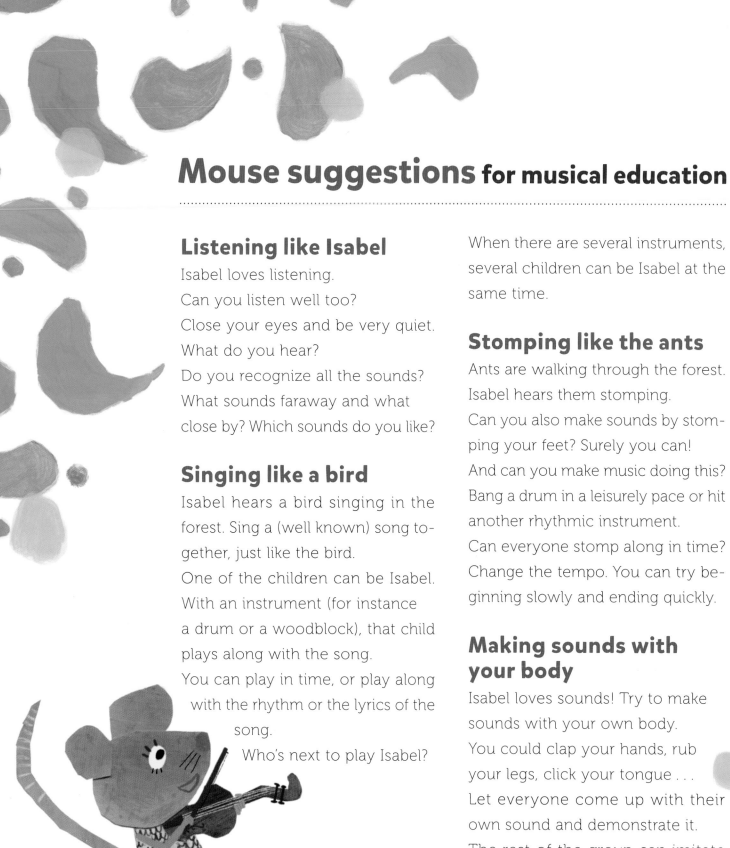